Busy Machines
Trucks

Written by Amy Johnson

Illustrated by Craig Shuttlewood

WINDMILL
BOOKS ™

Published in 2021 by Windmill Books,
an Imprint of Rosen Publishing
29 East 21st Street, New York, NY 10010

Copyright © 2021 by Miles Kelly Publishing

Find us on

Cataloging-in-Publication Data

Names: Johnson, Amy. | Shuttlewood, Craig.
Title: Trucks / Amy Johnson, illustrated by Craig Shuttlewood.
Description: New York : Windmill Books, 2021. | Series: Busy machines
Identifiers: ISBN 9781499485813 (pbk.) | ISBN 9781499485837 (library bound) | ISBN 9781499485820 (6 pack) | ISBN 9781499485844 (ebook)
Subjects: LCSH: Trucks--Juvenile literature.
Classification: LCC TL230.15 J66 2021 | DDC 629.224--dc23

Manufactured in the United States of America

CPSIA Compliance Information: Batch BS20WM: For Further Information contact Rosen Publishing, New York, New York at 1-800-237-9932

Out and about

The roads are busy with vehicles, big and small, carrying all kinds of loads. Many of them are trucks!

Flatbed truck

They THUNDER...

and TRUNDLE...

Pickup truck

Van

Semi

and GROWL!

Dump truck

3

Tremendous transporters

Rumbling along, these tough trucks
haul heavy cargo.

Long combination vehicle

Concrete mixer

Car carrier

4

Container truck

Fuel tanker

Low loader

5

Clearing the streets

Street sweepers have speedy spinning brushes that scrub away dirt and trash.

Spinning brush

WHOOSH!

When heavy snow hits, **snowplows** work to clear the way.

6

In cold weather, **salt trucks** spread salt on the roads to keep them from icing over.

Recycling trucks collect the things you put in your recycling bin.

7

Monster mayhem

Brightly painted trucks jump and spin, landing on giant tires — welcome to the **monster truck** show!

In races, two trucks race on tracks with sharp bends and big jumps.

Shock absorbers keep the truck body steady.

The trucks do stunts like wheelies and backflips.

The body is a big car or pickup truck.

Massive
off-road tires

9

All about semis

Semis are big vehicles that carry cargo over long distances. There's lots to be done before the semi sets out.

This semi has soft sides that can be opened like a curtain.

A forklift loads the cargo.

Cargo is kept inside the trailer.

The trailer is attached to a tractor unit.

The driver sits in the cab.

There is space inside the cab for drivers to rest and eat – they need to take breaks so they don't get too tired.

Powerful engine

11

Busy machines!

Delivery time

These hardworking vehicles are always on the go. They have plenty of deliveries to make!

The **postal van** has lots of packages and letters to be delivered.

The cargo area works like a giant fridge.

Refrigerated trucks keep things cold and transport food and drinks, such as fruit and milk.

14

A moving truck can be stacked high with furniture.

Milk trucks aren't used as much today, but you might have seen one!

Delivery trucks deliver things that people have ordered online.

Massive movers

High up in the mountains in Chile, two amazing trucks do a special job — they transport huge telescope antennas.

Each antenna weighs a lot! Moving them takes very powerful engines.

Each transporter truck is about the length of five small cars.

This transporter is called Lore. Its twin is named Otto.

Lore

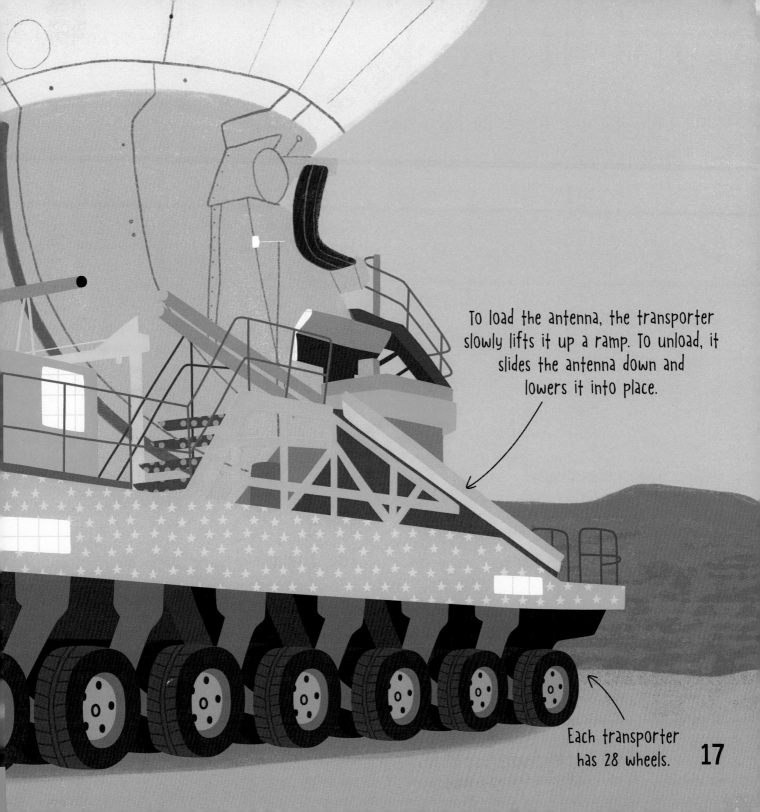

To load the antenna, the transporter slowly lifts it up a ramp. To unload, it slides the antenna down and lowers it into place.

Each transporter has 28 wheels.

17

Hard at work

Some vehicles are built to take on the toughest jobs, from hauling rocks to fighting fires.

All-terrain truck

Logging truck

Military truck

Fire engine

18

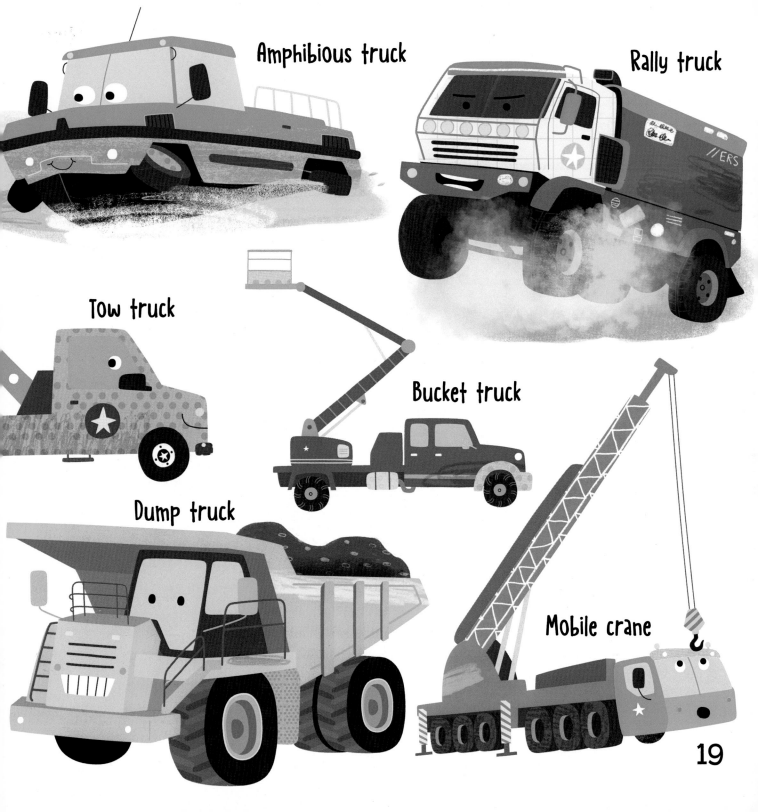

Amphibious truck

Rally truck

Tow truck

Bucket truck

Dump truck

Mobile crane

19

All about car carriers

With shiny new cars packed onto its decks, the towering **car carrier** is ready to go!

Some car carriers have room for 12 cars at once!

The carrier has ramps that can be lifted and tilted to fit the cars on.

To keep them safely in place, the cars are tied down by chains or straps.

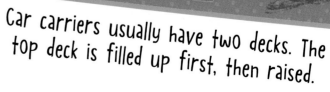

Car carriers usually have two decks. The top deck is filled up first, then raised.

21

Airport trucks

A plane has just landed – no time to lose! A team of hardworking trucks gets it ready for the next flight.

A **deicing truck** sprays a special mixture to melt any ice. Its arm can reach the top of the plane.

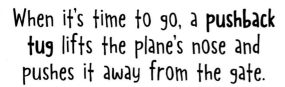

When it's time to go, a **pushback tug** lifts the plane's nose and pushes it away from the gate.

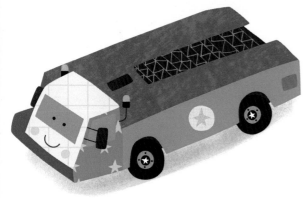

Mobile stairs are driven to the plane. Sometimes passengers use them.

Fuel is pumped into the plane by a **refueler**.

Luggage is driven to the plane on a **baggage truck**. It then goes up to the cargo hold on a **belt loader**.

Truck race!

It's time for the trucks to take to the track! They battle it out to be first to the finish.

We speed around the circuit, weaving past each other.

Races are usually 8 to 12 laps. The trucks zip around at up to 100 miles (160 km) per hour!